AF583393

family

AUNTY FAY MUIR & SUE LAWSON

ILLUSTRATED BY

JASMINE SEYMOUR

Family.
Heart and home.

Yarning old people,
endless sky,
breeze through silky oak.

Family.
Stories and songs.

Sharing how to care
for mob and Country.

Listening to Aunties,
Uncles, Elders and Ancestors.

Learning how to be –
to each other,
to Country.

Family.
Caring for twisting gum,
rushing river,

sighing sea.

Family.
Kinship that binds.
Showing the way.

Connecting
to ancestors,
to who we are,
to who
we will be.

Family.
Heart and home.

This is a Magabala Book
LEADING PUBLISHER OF ABORIGINAL AND TORRES STRAIT ISLANDER STORYTELLERS.
CHANGING THE WORLD, ONE STORY AT A TIME.

First published 2020, reprinted 2022, 2023
Magabala Books Aboriginal Corporation, Broome, Western Australia
W: www.magabala.com E: sales@magabala.com

Magabala Books receives financial assistance from the Commonwealth Government through the Australia Council, its arts advisory body.
The State of Western Australia has made an investment in this project through the Department of Local Government, Sport and Cultural Industries.
Magabala Books would like to acknowledge the support of the Shire of Broome, Western Australia.

Magabala Books is Australia's only independent Aboriginal and Torres Strait Islander publishing house. Magabala Books acknowledges the Traditional Owners of the Country on which we live and work. We recognise the unbroken connection to traditional lands, waters and cultures. Through what we publish, we honour all our Elders, peoples and stories, past, present and future.

Printed by Everbest Printing Ltd

The illustrations in this book are mixed media – created with monoprinting and digital compositions.

ISBN 978-1-925936-28-5

A catalogue record for this book is available from the National Library of Australia

Packaged by Ballantyne Rawlins in collaboration with Magabala Books.

OUR PLACE logo is made from original art by Lisa Kennedy.

For my niece and nephews and their children. Keeping the family connections strong!

F. S-M.

For Doobs – Dr Julianne Krusche – my dear friend, my partner in naughtiness and my rock.

S.L.

For my mudjin — my family.

J.S.

Fay Stewart-Muir is a Boonwurrung Elder who cares about sharing her First Nation culture and stories with all children to enjoy and take on a journey of learning.

Sue Lawson's award-winning young adult and children's books are recognised for the sensitive way they explore the exciting and heartbreaking complexities of growing up. Her first book with Aunty Fay was *Nganga: Aboriginal and Torres Strait Islander Words and Phrases*.

Jasmine Seymour is a Darug writer, artist and teacher. Her previous books are *Baby Business* and *Cooee Mittigar: A Story on Darug Songlines* with Leanne MulgoWatson, both published by Magabala Books.

The authors and illustrator wish to acknowledge that Family was written on Wadawurrung and illustrated on Darug people's land.